The Perfect Present

The Perfect Present

by ABBY KLEIN

illustrated by
JOHN MCKINLEY

Scholastic Inc.

New York   Toronto   London   Auckland

Sydney   Mexico City   New Delhi   Hong Kong

To my family,
Being with you makes my holiday perfect!

Lots of Love,
A. K.

No part of this publication may be reproduced, stored in a retrieval
system, or transmitted in any form or by any means, electronic,
mechanical, photocopying, recording, or otherwise, without written
permission of the publisher. For information regarding permission,
write to Scholastic Inc., Attention: Permissions Department,
557 Broadway, New York, NY 10012.

ISBN-13: 978-0-545-13043-1
ISBN-10: 0-545-13043-3

12 11 10 9 8 7 6 5 4 3   9 10 11 12 13 14/0

Printed in the U.S.A.
First printing, November 2009

CHAPTERS

I have a problem.

A really, really, big problem.

There are so many toys I want

for Christmas that I can't decide

which ones to put on my list.

Let me tell you about it.

CHAPTER 1

Making a List

"Only two more weeks until Christmas. I'd better start making my list," I said to my mom and dad.

"That's a good idea," my mom said. "Do you know what you want this year?"

"Boy, do I ever! I think I might need more than one piece of paper!"

"Really?" said my dad.

"Really!" I ran over to the desk in the kitchen and grabbed some paper and a pencil. "Can you help me write it? I'm not sure how to spell some of the words."

"Of course," said my mom. "What do you want to write first?"

"Umm . . . let me see. I think I want to write 'Video Funstation.'"

"Video Funstation?" said my sister, Suzie. "Do you know how much those cost? And they are almost impossible to get."

"So?"

"So," she said, "I wouldn't count on getting that. Everyone at school wants one, and none of the stores around here have any."

"I saw on the news last night that they get a few in every day, and you just have to wait in line," I said.

"A very long line," my dad interrupted.

"Yes," added my mom. "Some of the people waited in line for six hours only to find out that they were already gone."

"Aren't I worth it?" I said, flashing my cutest smile and giving my mom a big hug.

"Yeah, right," Suzie said, snickering. "I think I'm going to be sick."

"Suzie, that's not nice," said my dad. "Please don't talk about your brother that way."

"Fine," she mumbled. "But aren't you going to tell him that the Funstation is out of the question?"

"Are you his mother or father?" my dad asked her.

"Well . . . no."

"Then I suggest you let your mother and me worry about what is out of the question."

"Suzie," said my mom, "why don't you work on your own Christmas list? I'm sure there are things you want."

"Yes, there are."

"Then here's a piece of paper for you. You work on your own list, and we'll continue to help Freddy with his."

Suzie took the paper and moved down to the end of the table.

"If you really want the Funstation, then put it on your list," said my dad. "But remember that the things you put on your list are just suggestions for us and for Santa. There are no guarantees."

"I know, but I really want it, so I'll put it as number one on my list. That way you and Santa will know that it's my first choice."

"You do that," said my mom. "But first, don't forget to write your name at the top of the paper."

"Oh, I almost forgot," I said, giggling. "I wouldn't want to get my list mixed up with Suzie's."

"That's for sure," said Suzie. "I really don't want Commander Upchuck underpants for Christmas!"

"What kind of weirdo asks for underpants for Christmas?" I said.

"You! That's who!" Suzie said, laughing.

"That's not true! I have never put underpants on my Christmas list. I only put good stuff. You, on the other hand, put the lamest things."

"I do not!"

"Oh, yes you do."

"Really? Like what?"

"Like bubble-gum-pink nail polish and banana-split lip gloss."

"What's wrong with those?" asked my mom.

"They're not toys! That's what's wrong," I said. "On Christmas you are supposed to get toys, not makeup."

"Says who?" Suzie asked.

"Says me."

"Well, that's the dumbest thing I ever heard," said Suzie.

"All right, enough, you two," said my dad. "Suzie can put what she wants on her list, and, Freddy, you can put what you want on your list. But if the two of you continue to argue, then we will be done making lists! Understood?"

I nodded.

Suzie nodded.

"Good. The holidays are supposed to be a time for peace and happiness. Not for fighting."

I turned back to my paper and carefully printed "Freddy's Christmas List" at the top. Then I wrote a big number one. I wrote "V-I-D-E-O" and "F-U-N," but then I had to have my mom help me with the rest. When I was done writing it, I underlined it and put two stars next to the number one.

"There. I think you and Santa will know that I really want this."

"Yes, I think we all get the picture," my mom said, laughing. "Is that it? I thought you needed two pieces of paper because there were so many things that you wanted."

"Oh, I'm just getting started," I said, smiling. "Let's see. Number two: the new Backlot Baseball game for the Funstation. Robbie and I saw a commercial for it on TV yesterday, and it looks really cool. You can set up teams and play against your friends."

"That does sound fun," said my dad. "Can I play sometime?"

"Of course!" I said. "Number three: the new thresher shark's tooth I saw at Timeless Treasures at the mall. I definitely need that for my collection.

"Number four: the new *All About Sharks* video. It shows some really awesome shark attacks."

"Oh, Freddy," said my mom. "That is disgusting."

"Number five: a real baseball bat," I said. "If

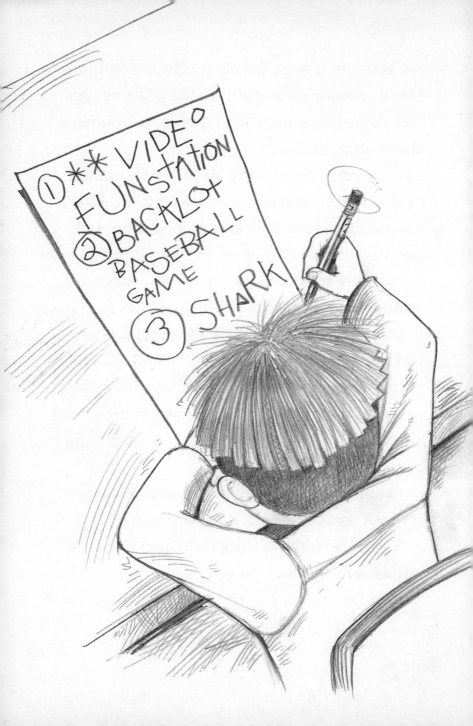

I'm going to play coach pitch this year in Little League, then I am going to need a good bat.

"Number six: the new Commander Upchuck laser sword. Those things are really cool. Max brought one to school the other day."

"I thought you weren't allowed to bring weapons to school," Suzie said, looking up from her list.

"You're not. As soon as he took it out of his backpack at recess, Mrs. Wushy took it away, and he got sent to the principal's office. But I got a good look at it, and it was awesome! Mom, how do you spell 'sword'?"

"It has a silent 'w' in it, honey. You spell it s-w-o-r-d."

"That's weird," I said.

"So are you almost done, Freddy?" my dad asked.

"Done? No way!" I chuckled. "I told you, Dad. My list is really long this year."

"Well, we don't have all night," said my mom.

I added numbers seven, eight, nine, and ten to my list, and then I had an idea. "Uh . . . I'll be back in a second," I said, getting out of my chair.

"Where are you going?" asked my mom.

"Uh . . . I just have to go up to my room for a second to check on the name of something," I called as I ran out of the room and up the stairs.

CHAPTER 2

The Present Detective

While I had been writing my list, a great idea had popped into my head. If I could figure out where my mom had hidden some of my presents, then I wouldn't have to put those on my list. I didn't want to write down things they had already bought. Why waste the space?

I sat down on my bed and hit my forehead with the palm of my hand. "Think, think, think."

I know . . . , I thought. *The laundry room! I*

never go in there, so it would be a good place for her to hide stuff. The only problem was that the laundry room was downstairs and my parents were in the kitchen. Trying to sneak down there would be too risky a mission right now. I'd have to do that sometime when my mom was taking a shower upstairs in her bathroom. She'd never hear me with the water running.

Her bathroom! That's it! The cupboard under the sink in her bathroom was the perfect hiding place. It was just full of lotions and soaps. I would never have any reason to go in there, so she probably thought that would be a good place to hide things. I smiled to myself. *You are so smart,* I thought.

I had to work fast. I didn't have a lot of time. If I was gone too long, then they would start looking for me.

Since this was a secret spy mission, I had to think like a spy. *Let's see . . . spies have to be super-quiet so no one hears them.* I looked down at my feet. I definitely had to take off my shoes. It would be harder for them to hear me walking around up there if I was just wearing my socks.

Hmmmm, what else? Oh yes! A flashlight, just in case I had to do some snooping in the dark. I opened the drawer of my nightstand and took out my sharkhead flashlight. I keep it right by my bed in case I need it in the middle of the night. I switched it on and off once just to make sure that the battery wasn't dead. "Perfect," I whispered.

I very quietly opened my door and tiptoed to the top of the stairs. I stood there for a minute, listening to what was going on in the kitchen. Suzie was talking to my parents about her Christmas list, so I had some time.

I tiptoed down the hall into my parents' bedroom and then into their bathroom. When I went to set my flashlight down, I accidentally knocked into my mom's glass perfume bottle. It spun around on the counter for a few seconds and then toppled off the edge. I reached my hand out and caught it just before it hit the bathroom floor.

"Boy, that was a close one," I whispered to myself. My mom is a neat freak, and that would have been a real mess. Besides, that perfume was a special present my grandparents had brought her from France. I would have been grounded for weeks!

After I gently set the bottle back on the counter, I decided just to leave my flashlight on the floor. I slowly opened the cupboard. My heart was beating wildly at the thought of what I was about to discover. It was so exciting.

I carefully pushed aside some toilet paper. Nothing. I pulled out some boxes of Kleenex that were stacked neatly in rows. Nothing. I felt around in the back of the cupboard with my hands. Nothing. Nothing. Nothing. Nothing.

"Bummer," I mumbled.

I had been so sure that I would find presents

in there that I didn't really have another plan.

Before I could look somewhere else, though, I would have to put everything back under the sink. I had to make sure I put each thing back in its exact place, or else my mom would know that someone had been doing something under there. I didn't want her to know I had been snooping around.

I stacked up the boxes of Kleenex and moved the toilet paper back into place. When everything was put away, I tiptoed into my parents' bedroom and shined my flashlight around it. Where else would be a good hiding place?

Aha! Their clothes closet. My mom loves clothes, so the closet is practically overflowing. She could shove things way in the back, and I would never see them, because they would be hidden by all the clothes hanging in there.

I had to open their closet door very slowly, because it always squeaked. I grabbed the handle and gently pulled.

This is a great hiding place. Why didn't I think of this the first time? I thought, smiling to myself. I had to be careful not to step on my mother's shoes. She has a gazillion pairs, and they are all lined up in perfect rows. I took out one pair and set them on the carpet. Then I knelt down in the empty space where the shoes had been and felt around with my hands in the back of the closet. Nothing. . . . Nothing. . . . I was starting to get really discouraged, and then . . .

Bingo!

I felt something long and skinny and hard, like a box. I grabbed my flashlight, pushed some of the clothes aside, and shined the light on the object in my hand. I had to bite my tongue so I wouldn't scream with excitement.

"Yes, yes, yes!" I whispered to myself. It was the remote-control diving shark I had seen at the aquarium. You can take it into the pool, and it can dive ten feet. My parents must have secretly bought it the last time we were there and put it

away for Christmas. Cool! Robbie and I would have fun with that all summer.

"I'm sure there must be more stuff in here," I whispered. I pushed aside my mom's fancy black party dress, and I couldn't believe my eyes.

There was the new Commander Upchuck Space Race computer game that Robbie and I played every time I went over to his house. I had been begging my mom for it for weeks! I picked it up and kissed it. "You're mine. You're mine. You're mine," I sang softly.

I carefully put it back in the same spot and was about to pick up something else I saw, behind my dad's pants, when something grabbed my leg from behind.

I froze.

CHAPTER 3

Gotcha!

"Hey, Shark Breath, what are you doing in there?" Suzie whispered.

Thank goodness it was only Suzie. If it had been my mom or dad, then I could probably kiss the Christmas presents good-bye.

I pulled my head out of the closet. "What am I doing in there?"

"Yeah. That's what I said. What are you doing in there?"

"Uh . . . nothing."

"Right," said Suzie. "Well, guess what? I don't believe you. And if you don't tell me the truth, then I'm going to go downstairs right now and tell Mom and Dad that you were snooping in their closet for Christmas presents."

"You wouldn't do that."

"Oh yeah? Watch me," she said as she started toward the door.

I pulled the rest of my body out of the closet and grabbed her arm. "Wait!"

"Are you going to tell me or not?"

"Do you promise not to tell Mom and Dad?"

"I don't know. What's it worth to you?"

I had to think fast. "How about you get the treats from the Advent calendar for the next two days?"

"Two days? I don't think so . . . more like I get the treats for a week," said Suzie.

"A week!"

"A week. Do we have a deal?" she asked, holding up her pinkie for a pinkie swear.

I love the treats from the Advent calendar, but I love Christmas presents more, so I decided that it was a good trade-off. "Fine," I said, holding up my pinkie.

We locked our fingers together.

"Deal," I said. "How did you know I was looking for Christmas presents?"

"Remember, I am two years older than you are, so I've had two more years to snoop around."

"Right," I said, laughing, "and you are one of the biggest busybodies."

"Hey," Suzie said. "Take that back, or I won't tell you about any of the other secret spots."

"There are other spots? Tell me! Tell me!" I said, jumping up and down.

"Shhhhh," said Suzie, "or we'll both get in trouble. We're not supposed to be in here, remember?"

"Sorry," I whispered.

Just then we heard my mom's voice from

downstairs. "Suzie . . . Freddy . . . what happened to you two?"

"Oh no," I whispered to Suzie. "We're gonna get it now!"

"Stop freaking out," she said. "Just hurry up and get those shoes back in the closet. We've got to get out of here fast!"

I carefully placed the shoes back in their spot and quietly closed the closet door. Then Suzie and I bolted out of the room and got into her room just as my mom reached the top of the stairs.

"Freddy . . . Suzie . . . Where are you two?"

"We're in my room, Mom," Suzie said.

"Oh, here you both are. What happened to you? Freddy, when you didn't come back down, Suzie went looking for you, but then she disappeared, too. I started to get worried."

"We're fine, Mom," Suzie said.

"Do you need any help?"

"That's okay, Mom," I said. "Suzie is helping me."

"Isn't that nice? I see the Christmas spirit has rubbed off on you two. By the way, did either of you go into my room? I thought I heard the floor creaking in there when I was downstairs."

Shoot! Suzie hadn't taken off her shoes! I swallowed hard and looked at Suzie. Then I mouthed, *We have a deal.*

Suzie nodded slightly. "Uh . . . yeah, Mom, that was me. I was in there looking for something."

I breathed a sigh of relief and mouthed, *Thank you.*

"What were you looking for?"

"That new Toy Crazy catalog. The one we were looking at the other day. Freddy and I had circled a bunch of things we wanted for Christmas."

"I don't think it's in my room, but I really can't remember where I last saw it."

"Freddy needed it because he was trying to remember what else he had wanted to add to his Christmas list."

"My goodness, Freddy!" my mom said, laughing. "Your list is so long already!"

"No, it's not, Mom. I'm just getting started."

"Ten things, and you're just getting started! Well, I think you are done at least for tonight. It's getting late."

"Aaaawwwww."

"I'll tell you what. I have to go to the mall tomorrow to get some presents for your cousins, so if you want, you can come along and pick up another copy of the Toy Crazy catalog from the store. They have a whole stack of them in there."

"Yippee!" I yelled, jumping on Suzie's bed and pumping my fist in the air. "I love going to the mall at Christmastime! I can't wait to see Santa."

"Freddy, get down off that bed this minute

before you break your neck!" my mom said.

"But I'm so excited!" I yelled.

"Well, Spaz," said Suzie, "go be excited in your own room. You're messing up my bed."

"Come on, Freddy," my mom said as she

helped me down. "It's time for you to get ready for bed."

"Aww, Mom, can't I stay up just a few more minutes?"

"Not if you want to come with me to the mall tomorrow. I want to get going early. It's always a nightmare trying to find parking there this time of year."

"All right," I said as I headed off to the bathroom to brush my teeth. "I wouldn't want to miss the trip to the mall. I can't wait to see all those toys, toys, toys, toys!"

CHAPTER 4

Ho, Ho, Ho

The next morning we got up early and went to the mall. It was so busy there that it took about ten minutes just to find a parking place.

"There's a spot, Dad. Grab it before someone else does!"

"Calm down, Freddy. I see it," said my dad, pulling into the space.

As soon as he turned off the engine, I jumped out of the car. "Come on! Come on, everybody. Let's go!"

"Aren't you an eager beaver this morning?" said my mom.

"More like an annoying pain," said Suzie.

"Seriously, Freddy," said my dad, "what's the rush? I, for one, am not looking forward to shopping today. The mall is going to be really crowded and the lines are going to be long."

"Aww, Dad, don't be so grumpy. It's the season of joy and happiness."

"You tell him, Freddy," my mom said, laughing. "Maybe we should start calling your dad the Grinch."

"Very funny," said my dad.

We walked across the parking lot and into the mall. It was packed with people.

"Isn't it great?" I said. "The lights, the decorations, the holiday music . . . and look! There's Santa!"

I started dragging my mom in that direction. "Mom! Mom!" I yelled, jumping up and down. "Can I go sit on Santa's lap and tell him what I want for Christmas?"

"From the looks of your Christmas list, I don't think there are enough hours in the day!" my dad said, chuckling.

I ignored him. "Pleeeeease, Mom. Pretty please with a cherry on top?" I said, giving her my sad puppy-dog face.

"I know you want to talk to Santa, Freddy, but right now there are about fifteen kids in line. How about if we do some of our shopping, and then come back later?"

I stuck out my lower lip in a big pout.

"Oh, what's that?" said my dad. "Are you pouting? You know what they say about Santa: 'You better not pout, better not cry, Santa Claus is coming to town.' I don't think he brings presents to kids who are pouting."

I quickly glanced in Santa's direction to make

sure he hadn't seen me pouting, and then I put a big smile on my face. "Pouting? Who's pouting?" I said, grinning.

"That's better," said my mom.

"So, can I talk to Santa? I have to make sure he knows I want that Funstation."

"Oh all right," said my mom. "Let's get in line."

We joined the line that seemed to be getting longer by the minute.

"I can't believe that Santa can make toys for

all the children in the whole world," I said.

"He is a pretty special guy," said my mom.

"I wish I could travel to the North Pole one day and visit Santa's workshop. That would be so cool. How many elves do you think work for Santa Claus?"

"Thousands," Suzie said.

"Really?"

"Really. How else would Santa be able to make all those toys in one year?"

"That's true."

"This line is taking forever," Suzie whined.

"It shouldn't be too much longer," said my

mom. "It's actually moving pretty quickly."

"It won't when I get up there," I said, laughing. "I have so many things to tell Santa that I want."

"What makes you so sure you are going to get anything from Santa?" asked Suzie.

"What do you mean?"

"Santa doesn't bring things to kids who have been naughty."

"I have been really good all year."

"Yeah, right," Suzie said, snickering.

I was going to say something back to her, but I bit my tongue. I didn't want Santa to see me

arguing with my sister. If he saw us fighting, then I definitely wouldn't end up on the Nice List.

"Only three more people and then it's our turn," I said excitedly. "I can't wait! I can't wait!"

"Calm down, Hammerhead," Suzie whispered. "You're embarrassing me."

"Oh, Suzie," said my dad. "He's just excited."

"Next!" Santa's elf called, pointing to me. "It's your turn."

I ran up to Santa Claus. "Hi, Santa," I said.

"Ho, ho, ho. Well, hello there. What's your name?"

"Freddy."

"Nice to meet you, Freddy. Would you like to come sit on my lap and tell me what you want for Christmas?"

"Yes!" I said, and jumped up on his lap.

"Now tell old Santa what you'd like me to bring you."

"Well, Santa, I really, really, really want a Funstation."

"It seems a lot of children want that this year."

"I know. That's why there aren't any left in the stores. But I told all my friends not to worry, because Santa would bring it to us."

"Ho, ho, ho. I have my elves working around the clock trying to make enough Funstations for all the boys and girls."

"I knew it," I said, grinning.

"Is there anything else you want, Freddy?"

"Oh yes, Santa. I already have ten things on my list, and I have more things to add."

"Ten things! I won't be able to remember them all, so why don't you just send me a letter at the North Pole. Mrs. Claus reads all the letters and lets me know what every child wants."

"Okay, I'll do that. I just have to add a few more things before I send it."

"Ho, ho, ho. Nice to meet you, Freddy. I hope

you have a merry Christmas. Now, smile big. One of my elves is going to take our picture."

I grabbed Santa's hand and smiled.

Click went the camera. "Great one!" said the elf.

"Here's a little treat for you," said Santa, and he handed me a candy cane.

"Thanks, Santa. I hope you have a very merry Christmas, too!"

I jumped off his lap and ran over to my family. "I just love Santa. I think Christmas is my favorite holiday!" I said, smiling.

CHAPTER 5

Toy Crazy

"Now come on," said my mom. "I want to get to the toy store before they sell out of that Niki doll your cousin Ashley wants. I heard they only have a few left."

"Remember, I want one of those, too," said Suzie. "Maybe you should buy two of them today, before they are all gone."

"Nice try," said my dad.

"What?" said Suzie. "It was just a suggestion."

"You two are so focused on what *you're* going to get. You know Christmas isn't just about getting presents," said my mom. "Where's your spirit of giving?"

"But the best part of Christmas is all the toys you get!" I said.

My mom sighed. "What am I going to do with you, Freddy?"

Just then the song "Jingle Bells" started to play, and I sang along. "Jingle Bells, Batman smells, Robin laid an egg. . . ."

"Freddy? What are you singing?" my mom asked.

"'Jingle Bells.'"

"That's not 'Jingle Bells.'"

"It's the way everyone at school sings it."

"Well, I like the real version, so if you are going to sing along, would you please sing the version our family sings on Christmas Eve?"

"Oh all right. But that version isn't as funny."

We kept walking and I hummed "Jingle Bells" while I sang the silly version to myself in my head.

Finally we got to the Toy Crazy store. The line was out the door.

"What did I tell you?" my dad said. "Just look at this line!"

"Well, Mr. Grinch, we don't have a choice," said my mom. "I have to get Ashley that doll."

When we walked inside, I noticed a Christmas tree decorated with paper ornaments that had pictures of toys on them. As people walked by, they were picking the ornaments off the tree, walking up to the cash register, and saying, "I'd like this one, please."

"Cool. Look!" I said. "You get to pick a free toy today. Can I get one, Mom? Can I? Can I?"

"What are you talking about, Freddy?" said my mom.

"See that tree over there?"

"Yes."

"People are taking an ornament off the tree, walking to the front, and telling the person who works here that they want that toy."

"Freddy," my mom said, "those people are not getting those toys for themselves, and the toys are not free."

"They're not?"

"No, they are buying those toys for other children who don't get a lot of toys at Christmas."

"Bummer. I thought they were free. There was some pretty cool stuff hanging on that tree."

"Here we are," said my mom as we turned down the doll aisle. "Now, where is that Niki doll?"

This is no fun, I thought. *I won't be able to find more toys to add to my Christmas list in the doll aisle.*

"I don't see it," my mom said. "I hope they haven't sold out!"

"It should be right here," said my dad. "That's where the label on the shelf is."

"I know," said my mom, "but there's just a big empty space. No dolls."

All of a sudden Suzie yelled, "I found one! I found one!"

We looked over, and she was waving the box with the Niki doll in the air.

"Where did you find that?" asked my mom.

"I found it hidden behind a bunch of other dolls," Suzie said. "Way on the back of the shelf."

"I wonder how it got there."

"I know how it got there," said Suzie. "It's an old trick that kids do. If we want a toy, but our mom and dad won't let us get it, then we hide it behind other toys, so that other kids won't see it, and then we hope that one day when we can come back to buy it, it will still be there."

"Wow! That's interesting. I never knew that," my dad said, smiling.

"It's true," I said. "All the kids do it. Now that you found it, can I go look in the boys' section?"

"Just for a minute, while Mom is paying," said

my dad. "Then we have to leave. It's crazy in here!"

My dad followed me into the boys' section. "Stay close to me, Freddy. There are so many people in here. I don't want you to get lost!"

"Look, Dad!" I shouted. "There's the new Commander Upchuck Super Space Flyer. Can you get it down, so I can look at it?"

My dad took the box down from the shelf and handed it to me.

"Wow! This is really cool, Dad. The spaceship is remote control, and Commander Upchuck and Cookie fit right inside. You can actually make them fly!"

"It's very expensive, Freddy."

"How much?"

"Fifty dollars."

"That's okay. I'll just add it to my Christmas list," I said, smiling.

I turned the corner and walked down the next aisle. "I can't believe it," I said.

"What?" said my dad.

"They have a hammerhead shark model you can build." I grabbed the box off the shelf. "It comes with all the pieces to make your very own hammerhead shark. I've never seen this before. I just have to have it. I'll add it to the list."

"I think your list is getting a little out of control," said my dad.

Just then my mom and Suzie found us. "Now I know why they call this store Toy Crazy," said my mom. "It's crazy in here! Let's get out of here before we get crushed!"

"Or before Freddy finds one more thing to add to his Christmas list," said my dad.

He grabbed my hand, and we made our way out of the store, but not before I picked up a copy of the Toy Crazy catalog so I could add more cool toys to my list.

CHAPTER 6

Holiday Wishes

The next day, during lunchtime at school, my friends and I were all talking about what we wanted for the holidays.

"Hey, Robbie," I said. "I saw that new Commander Upchuck Super Space Flyer yesterday at Toy Crazy."

"You did? Is it as cool as it looks on TV?"

"Even cooler," I said. "The remote control has all kinds of different buttons and your Commander Upchuck and Cookie action figures both fit inside. You can actually make them fly."

"No way!" said Robbie. "That is really cool. I think I'm going to add that to my Kwanzaa list."

"I already added it to my list," I said, giving Robbie a high five.

"What are you two dorks talking about adding to your lists?" Max butted in. "Pink tutus?"

"Uhhh . . . uhhh . . . ," I stammered.

"Do you need those for ballet class?" Max said, laughing hysterically.

"I need a tutu for *my* ballet class," said Chloe. "My nana bought me one that is pink with silver sparkles all over it."

"Was I talking to you?" Max barked in her face.

"Well, no . . . but . . ."

"Then stop talking. That's all you do: talk, talk, talk."

"He is so mean," I whispered to Robbie.

Max whipped his head around and slowly stood up. "What did you say, Pipsqueak?"

I swallowed hard. He wasn't supposed to hear that. Now what was I going to do? The biggest bully in the whole first grade looked like he was about to hurt me.

Jessie tapped Max on the shoulder. "I'll tell you what he said. He said you're really mean."

Jessie was so brave. She was the only one who wasn't afraid to stand up to Max.

"They don't have pink tutus on *their* lists," Jessie continued, "but I bet you have one on yours."

We all started laughing and Max's face turned bright red. He sat back down and took another bite of his sandwich.

"Thanks, Jessie," I said.

"No problem. That's what friends do. They stick up for each other," she said, smiling.

"What do you have on your Christmas list?" I asked.

"A few things," said Jessie.

"A few things! I have so many things on my list I don't even remember how many there are!" I said.

"Well, I have three lists," said Chloe, holding up three fingers with painted red fingernails. "One for my parents, one for my nana, and one for Santa."

"Big deal. I have four lists," Max bragged.

"You do not!" said Chloe.

"Oh yes I do!" shouted Max.

"Do not!"

"Do too!" Max said as he yanked one of Chloe's fiery red curls.

"Ouch! You hurt me! You hurt me!" Chloe wailed. "I'm going to tell Miss Becky on you."

She left to get Miss Becky, the lunch teacher.

When everything was quiet again at the table, Jessie said, "Every Christmas my mom, my grandma, and I give away a lot of presents."

"Really?" I said.

"Really. When my grandma, my *abuela*, was a little girl growing up in Mexico, her parents were very poor. They could never afford to buy her a present for Christmas. But every year a neighbor gave her a present at the *Las Posadas* party. Those presents were always really special to my grandma, so every year at holiday time, she reminds me to help other people and not just think of myself and what I want."

"Who do you give the presents to?" I asked.

"Kids at the homeless shelter. Families from my church. We even send some to children in Mexico."

"But don't those kids get stuff from Santa?"

"Yes, but they don't get anything from their mom and dad because their parents don't have enough money to buy them something they really want."

"That's sad," I said.

"Yes, it is," said Jessie. "Christmas is supposed to be a happy time, but for some kids, it's not."

"How do you do it?" I asked.

"Do what?" said Jessie.

"Give those kids presents."

"Have you ever seen those big huge bins full of toys at the mall?"

"I saw a bunch the other day," Robbie said.

"You can buy a toy and drop it in that bin, and then people make sure that those toys go to kids who need them."

"Yesterday when I was in Toy Crazy, I saw people taking these little ornaments that had pictures of toys on them off a tree. Then they would go to the cash register and tell the person working there that they wanted that toy. I thought they were giving away free toys, but my mom told me that those people were actually buying toys for other kids. I didn't really understand what she was saying, but now I think I do," I said.

"Oh yeah!" said Robbie. "I saw that, too."

"Some stores do that," said Jessie. "It's like a wishing tree. Kids at the homeless shelter will tell someone what they really want for the holidays, and then the store will hang a picture of that wish on a tree. Anyone can come along and buy that toy and make that kid's wish come true."

"I want to make a kid's holiday wish come true," I said.

"Me, too!" said Robbie.

"It's easy," said Jessie. "And when you do it, you'll feel really good inside."

CHAPTER 7

Making Another List

When I got home from school, I decided to change my Christmas list. But first I had to find it, because my mom and dad had put it away somewhere. They didn't want me adding anything else to it.

I left my backpack by the door and walked into the kitchen.

"Freddy? Is that you?" my mom called from the laundry room.

"Yeah, Mom, it's me."

"I'll be right there. I just have to finish folding the laundry."

"Take your time!" I yelled back. "Actually, take all the time you want," I mumbled to myself.

I looked around the room. Where would she put that list? I wondered.

I decided to check the junk drawer first. Sometimes my dad shoves things in there. Nope, it wasn't there.

Next I checked the mail holder. I found my karate schedule and a letter from my school, but no Christmas list.

I opened the small desk drawer and lifted a few papers, but I still could not find that list! I was just shutting the drawer when my mom walked into the room.

"Looking for something?" she asked.

"Uhhh . . . just a new pencil for my homework."

"You should have just asked me, honey. I

would have been happy to get it for you," my
mom said.

"I didn't want to bother you while you were
folding laundry, and I wanted to get started on
my homework right away."

"How about a snack first?"

"Nah. I'm not that hungry. I think I'll just go
upstairs and get to work."

"I've never seen you so eager to do your homework," said my mom. "It must be a fun assignment."

"Yeah. Yeah, it is," I said. "Lots of fun. I just need a pencil."

"Sure thing," said my mom. "I actually just bought some new ones the other day. You and Suzie go through pencils so fast that I would swear you two are eating them!"

"Very funny, Mom," I said.

"Well, here you go," she said, handing me a brand-new pencil. "I even sharpened it for you." "Thanks, Mom. I'll be up in my room."

"Just call me if you need any help. I'm going to stay down here and start making dinner."

"Okay, Mom," I said as I started to leave the room. "Don't worry about me. I'm off to work."

I picked up my backpack and climbed the stairs to my room. I dropped my backpack on the floor, kicked off my shoes, and tiptoed down the hall to my parents' room. I just had to find that Christmas list. If it was not in the kitchen, then it must be in their room somewhere.

I looked around the room. I didn't have a lot of time to waste. My mom might walk up the stairs any minute to check on me, and even worse, Suzie would be coming home from ballet soon, and she always had to know what I was up to. She really was the biggest busybody on the planet!

I hit my forehead with the palm of my hand. "Think, think, think!"

One time I had seen my mom pull a paper out of the drawer in her nightstand. I tiptoed over and gently pulled the drawer open. I saw her reading glasses and a book, the one she reads every night before bed. I carefully lifted the book, and there it was! My Christmas list!

"Got it!" I whispered to myself. I quietly shut the drawer, tiptoed to their bedroom door, and stuck my head out. The coast was clear, so I went back to my bedroom and shut the door.

I lay down on my bed and looked over my list. "Yep, I definitely have to make some changes," I said to myself.

I took out the pencil my mom had given me and erased a bunch of stuff. Then I added some new things: a Monster Mashers video game, a Sounds-n-Lights Fire Truck, and a Commander Upchuck Space Laser.

I was just about to add something else when my bedroom door flew open. It was Suzie. I shoved the list and the pencil under my stomach and lay on top of them.

"Hey, Shark Breath, did you take my new pencil?"

"No! Now get out of here, and next time don't forget to knock!"

Instead of leaving the room, Suzie walked closer to the bed.

"Get out of here!" I said.

"Not until you give me that pencil."

"It's not your pencil. Mom just gave it to me a few minutes ago."

"I don't believe you," she said. "I'll just have to see for myself."

She shoved her hand under my stomach to try to grab the pencil, and she touched the paper. "Why are you lying on a piece of paper?"

"I'm not."

"Oh yes you are. I could feel it."

"None of your business."

"Is it a love note for your girlfriend?"

"No. I don't have a girlfriend, and it is not a love note. Now leave me alone!"

"Not until you show me that paper."

"Leave me alone!" I screamed.

I guess I yelled a little too loudly, because my mom came running up the stairs and into my room. "What's going on up here? Are you all right, Freddy?"

"Freddy is hiding a piece of paper under his stomach," said Suzie.

"He's just working on his homework," said my mom.

"Oh no he's not. He's trying to hide something."

"Don't be silly, Suzie. He's not hiding anything."

"Really? Then ask him to roll over, Mom."

"Roll over?" my mom said, laughing. "Freddy's not a dog."

I giggled. "Yeah, I'm not a dog."

Before I knew what was happening, Suzie grabbed for the paper one more time and gave

a big tug. The paper ripped, and when I looked up, Suzie was holding a piece of my Christmas list in her hand.

"See, Mom? What did I tell you? This isn't his homework. This is Freddy's Christmas list!"

I looked at Suzie. Then I looked over at my mom.

"Freddy!" said my mom. "Where did you get this?"

I broke down crying. "I . . . I . . . ," I sobbed.

"Freddy, I am asking you a question."

"I . . . got . . . it . . . from . . . your . . . room," I said, choking back sobs.

"Oooooh, you are in so much trouble," said Suzie.

"Suzie," said my mom, "you need to go to your room. I need to talk to Freddy alone."

"But . . ."

"No buts. Now go!"

Suzie turned and marched out of the room.

"Now, Freddy," said my mom, "I thought I told

you that you were done with your Christmas list."

"I know!" I cried.

"Then why did you sneak into my room and take it?"

"I . . . just . . . had . . . to . . . add . . . a . . . few . . . more . . . things. . . ."

"But didn't Daddy and I tell you that you were not allowed to add anything else to the list?"

"Yes," I said, sniffling.

"You have way too many things on your list already. And look at what you added: a Monster Mashers video game? I thought those monsters gave you nightmares. A Sounds-n-Lights Fire Truck? You never play with trucks. And a Commander Upchuck Space Laser? You already have two of those! Now you are just getting greedy! I'm really disappointed in you, Freddy. You know Christmas is supposed to be a time of giving. You seem to have forgotten that."

"But that new stuff isn't for me," I whispered.

"What did you say?"

I sat up on my bed. "That new stuff I added today isn't for me, Mom."

"It's not? Then who is it for?"

"It's for the kids at the homeless shelter."

"The homeless shelter?"

"Yes. Today at school Jessie told me about

how every year her family buys toys for kids whose moms and dads can't buy them anything for Christmas. She said it's like making their wish come true. I wanted to make a kid's wish come true, but I didn't have enough money in my piggy bank, so I thought I could just add some more toys to my Christmas list and then give those toys away to kids who really needed them."

"Wow, Freddy! That is a wonderful thing to do," my mom said, giving me a great big hug.

"And if you look carefully, Mom, you'll see I erased a bunch of the toys for me. I don't want them anymore. I want to give toys away instead."

"I have definitely changed my mind, Freddy," said my mom. "I think you really do understand that the holidays are not just about what you can get, but what you can give to others."

"I really do want to make a kid's wish come true."

"I'll tell you what," said my mom. "How about if I take you and Suzie to the mall tomorrow, and you can each pick an ornament off the tree at Toy Crazy, and we'll donate those toys to children at the shelter. How does that sound?"

"That sounds great! Thanks, Mom," I said, giving her a big hug. "I am going to pick the perfect present."

CHAPTER 8

A Wish Come True

The next day, after school, my mom took Suzie and me to the mall. "Come on, Mom, can you walk a little faster?" I said as we made our way to Toy Crazy.

"I'm coming. I'm coming. You and Suzie can run ahead. I'll be right there."

I grabbed Suzie's hand, and the two of us ran down to the toy store. "It's right over here," I said to Suzie, bringing her to the present tree.

"See all these ornaments with pictures of toys on them?"

"Yeah."

"You pick the one you want, take it up to the cash register, and tell the lady that you want to buy that toy for a kid in the shelter."

"Oh, I get it," Suzie said. "That sounds like fun."

"It's going to be really hard to choose," I said.

"Hello, you two," said my mom. "Have you picked one out yet?"

"Picked one out?" I said, laughing. "We just got here, Mom."

"And there are so many to choose from," Suzie said.

"I think it's going to take me a long time," I said. "I want to look at all of the choices. I have to pick the perfect present."

"All right, Freddy," my mom said. "Take your time."

I walked slowly around the tree, looking at each picture very carefully.

"Ooooh, it's going to be so hard to decide," I said.

"I know what you mean," said Suzie.

"I like this Commander Upchuck action figure," I said, pointing to one of the pictures.

"You have one like that at home, don't you, Freddy?" my mom asked.

"Yes I do, and I love playing with it."

I grabbed another picture. "This space laser is really cool, too. Robbie and I play with these all the time.

"Oh, and look at this!" I said. "It's one of those marble-run games where you build a track and then drop the marble down and watch it go."

"I bet the child at the shelter will be happy with whatever you pick," my mom said.

"I'm trying to decide between this art kit and this doll," Suzie said.

"I think you should get the art kit," I said.

"The girl who gets it can make all kinds of cool stuff with it."

"What are you going to choose, Freddy?" Suzie asked.

"I'm not sure yet," I said.

"I think you should get the marble game. The kid who gets it can play it with other kids from the shelter."

"That's true," I said. "I just don't want to make the wrong choice."

"There is no such thing as the wrong choice," said my mom. "When you give something from your heart, it's always the right choice. And besides, the kids have picked these toys out already—you'll be giving them exactly what they want."

"I'm going to choose the art kit," Suzie said, taking that ornament off the tree.

"You are going to make a little girl very happy," said my mom. "And how about you, Freddy? What are you going to choose?"

"Ummm . . . ummm . . . I guess I'll choose the . . . the . . . marble game," I said, pulling off that ornament.

"Excellent choice!" said my mom. "Let's go pay for them."

We all walked up to the cash register.

"I would like to buy this toy for a kid at the homeless shelter," I said, handing the lady my choice.

"Well, aren't you a nice young man?" said the lady. "I know a child at the shelter is going to have a very merry Christmas because of you."

"I hope this is the perfect present," I said.

"Of course it's perfect," said the lady. "You know why? Because you picked it out, and you're giving it with love. The holidays are a time to think of others, not just ourselves, and you are doing just that. It seems that lately too many people are forgetting the true meaning of Christmas."

We paid for both presents and walked out of the store.

"Can we do this every year, Mom?" I asked.

"Of course, Freddy. I think this will be a new family tradition," my mom said.

"I think this is already the best Christmas ever!" I said. "And Santa hasn't even come yet!"

"Merry Christmas, kids," my mom said.

"Merry Christmas!"

DEAR READER,

Each year in December my family participates in the Adopt-A-Family Program. We are given a wish list from a family who cannot afford to buy their children the gifts they want for the holidays. Then my children, my husband, and I go out and buy them the things they wish for. There are local Adopt-A-Family organizations all over the country, and probably one near you if you want to get involved!

We have so much fun going to the mall and looking around for the perfect teddy bear or the warmest winter coat that we hope will make our "adopted" child happy. It has become one of our favorite holiday activities.

It is important to remember that the holidays are about giving, not just receiving. We must think of ways that we can help others celebrate the season and have the happiest of holidays.

I'm sure you have some great ideas about how to help others at the holiday time. I would love to hear about them. Just write to me at:

Ready, Freddy! Fun Stuff

c/o Scholastic Inc.

P.O. Box 711

New York, NY 10013-0711

I hope you had as much fun reading *The Perfect Present* as I had writing it.

HAPPY HOLIDAYS AND HAPPY READING!

Abby Klein

Freddy's Fun Pages

FREDDY'S SHARK JOURNAL

SHARKS THAT LIGHT UP

We put up lights to decorate for the holidays. Did you know that deep-water sharks make their own light?

Some sharks that live in deep water have special ways of making their own light.

The mouth of the megamouth shark shines with a silvery glow. The glow attracts the plankton that the megamouth likes to eat.

The belly of the cookiecutter shark glows a luminous green. Some animals, such as whales, are attracted to the light, and when they swim close by, the cookiecutter shark takes a bite!

Lantern fish are covered in a slime that glows in the dark. They swim in large schools, and scientists think that the slime helps the sharks keep their place in the school.

REINDEER CANDY CANES

Join in Freddy's spirit of giving and
make these sweet treats to give to
your friends at the holidays.

YOU WILL NEED:

candy canes
red and green pom-poms
brown pipe cleaners
small googly eyes
craft glue

1. Glue a pom-pom
onto the curved end of
a candy cane.

2. Glue two googly
eyes onto the curve of
the candy cane.

3. Twist a brown pipe
cleaner around the top of the
curve to make the antlers.

4. Give the reindeer candy
canes to your friends and
watch them smile!

HOLIDAY COUNTDOWN CHAIN

Are you as excited about the holidays as Freddy is? Make one of these paper chains and count down the days until your holiday starts!

YOU WILL NEED:

colored construction paper (appropriate colors for your holiday)
tape
scissors

1. Cut the colored construction paper into one-inch strips.

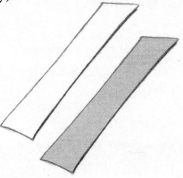

2. Take one strip and tape the two ends together to make a loop.

3. Stick another strip through the center of the first loop and tape those two ends together.

4. Continue connecting loops to your chain until you have one loop for each day from now until the start of your holiday.

5. Once your holiday countdown chain is complete, remove one loop from your chain each day until you have none left.

HAPPY HOLIDAYS!

HOLIDAY WORD SEARCH

Can you find these words hidden in the word search? The words may be hidden across, down, and diagonally. Good luck!

KWANZAA   MENORAH   HANUKKAH
DREIDEL   CHRISTMAS   WREATH
GIFT   KINARA   LIGHTS
TREE   SANTA   CELEBRATE

```
H A R O N E M N I F
M T L I G H T S H S
A N A S X O L A K A
T A W E K B N D I M
F S Z R R U S R N T
I J A N K W H E A S
G H L K A E T I R I
S O A V E W O D A R
B H W R G F K E Z H
A E T A R B E L E C
```

Have you read all about Freddy?

Don't miss any of Freddy's funny adventures!